Beauty
AND THE
Beaks

A TURKEY'S CAUTIONARY TALE

MARY JANE
AND
HERM AUCH

Holiday House
New York

This book is dedicated to our metal artist son, Ian,
who fabricated the chicken-sized
beauty parlor chair for The Chic Hen.

MARY JANE made the chicken mannequins with needle-felted wool wings and yarn hand
feathers. She sculpted a variety of polymer clay eyes and beaks for each bird, designed
and sewed the outfits, and sculpted the shoes from polymer clay.
HERM designed and built the sets from found and constructed objects. He made
a miniature photo studio with movable lights. After photographing and scanning
all the elements into his computer, he scaled them to fit the scenes.

Text copyright © 2007 by Mary Jane Auch
Illustrations copyright © 2007 by
Mary Jane and Herm Auch
All Rights Reserved
Printed and Bound in Malaysia
www.holidayhouse.com
First Edition
1 3 5 7 9 10 8 6 4 2

Library of Congress Cataloging-in-Publication Data
Auch, Mary Jane
Beauty and the beaks / by Mary Jane Auch ;
illustrated by Mary Jane and Herm Auch.
p. cm.
Summary: When Lance, a very pretentious turkey, arrives
on the farm and boasts that he is the only bird invited
to a special feast, no hen is impressed, but when Beauty learns
that Lance is the main course, she convinces the others to save him.
ISBN-13: 978-0-8234-1990-6
[1. Chickens—Fiction. 2. Turkeys—Fiction.
3. Thanksgiving Day—Fiction. 4. Humorous stories.] I. Auch, Herm, ill. II. Title.
PZ7.A898Bea 2007
[E]—dc22
2006049468

Designed by John Grandits

Chicksticks

IN 6

BEAKOMING

COLORS

E
AUCH

Appointments

8:00
8:30
9:00
9:30 Matilda / Touch up
10:00
10:30
11:00
11:30
12:00 Lucille / pedicure
12:30
1:00
1:30
2:00 Hattie / Trim
2:30
3:00
3:30 MJ / eggstreme makeover
4:00

The
Chic Hen

Everything to make you
a new chick

Beauty owned a beauty shop, The Chic Hen, where she made other chickens look their best. Though Beauty didn't encourage it, the shop was the center of gossip, with chicken beaks clicking all day.

The Chic Hen

OPEN

In her spare time, Beauty practiced her favorite eggsercise—flying. She was the only chicken on the farm who could soar over the fence. She didn't do it to run away. She flew for the pure joy of eggsploring.

One day a new bird arrived. "There's a chicken who could use a little sprucing up," clucked Beauty. "That hen needs eggstensive work!" squawked Beauty's assistant, Gladys.

"Hush," said Beauty, "you'll hurt her feelings."

But it was too late. "My name is Lance," said the bird.
"I'm not a hen. I'm a turkey." Lance strutted around the shop.
"I'm here for a special feast."

"We haven't heard anything about a feast," said Beauty.

Lance shook his wattle. "I guess you're not invited
then." And he swaggered out.

EGGSIT

"Some nerve!" huffed Gladys.

"Don't let his words stick in your gizzard," said Beauty. "Let's get to work."

Hattie came in for a trim, Matilda needed to touch up her feather color, and Lucille wanted a set and a pedicure. They had all heard about the feast, but none of them were invited either.

Eggsactly what the fashionable chicken will wear to the fowl ball. She'll be a vision in gold lamé.

This sea... bride steps in silver boo... and a polka-d... confection of a... gow...

Just then Lance came back. "This feast is a very eggsclusive event. There's only one bird invited. Me!" And he made another pretentious eggsit.

"I'm glad I'm not invited if he's going to be there," said Matilda.

"He is a bit self-centered," Beauty agreed, as she gave Lucille a comb-out.

"I'll find out about this feast," said Beauty. She flew to the farmhouse and peeked inside. The pantry shelves were filled with pies. "Lance was right about a feast. But with all those pies, he can't be the only guest."

Beauty's heart stopped when she saw a cookbook on the counter. "Roast turkey with chestnut stuffing? Poor Lance!"

Roast Turkey with Chestnut Stuffing

1 nice plump turkey

Stuffing – mix:
3 cups chopped chestnuts
1 cup onions
1 cup celery
3 cups stale bread cut in cubes
¼ cup chopped fresh sage
2 teaspoons salt
¼ teaspoon pepper

Stuff inside turkey.
Roast at 350° until internal temperature is 165°.

"Lance," cried Beauty. "You're going to be stuffed with chestnuts at the feast."

"Chestnuts? Yum!" said Lance. "What else is on the menu?"

"You!" exclaimed Beauty. "You *are* the feast."

"Wattle I do?" Lance wailed.

"Calm down," Beauty said. "I'll teach you to fly over the fence."

But in spite of his brawny drumsticks, Lance wasn't good at running, and he couldn't flap his burly wings fast enough to get off the ground.

"We'll make a hen ladder for you," said Beauty. She convinced her friends to cooperate. Gladys stayed at the bottom to push.

"Reach for me, Lance!" called Beauty. Lance tried but missed.

"Give him a boost, Gladys."

"He's not budging."

Gladys gave a mighty shove. The hen ladder collapsed.

"My life is about to eggspire!" blubbered Lance.

"Don't chicken out now," said Beauty. "We'll hide you."

"Are you yolking?" squawked Gladys. "He's too big to hide."

But Beauty was hatching a plan.
"Lance, come with me. You too, Gladys."
When they got to The Chic Hen,
Beauty announced, "Lance, we're giving
you an eggstreme makeover."

"Making this turkey look pretty won't save him," said Gladys. "No, we'll make him look like a hen. First we need to improve his complexion. No healthy hen has blue skin with red lumps."

They tried a mud pack with a cucumber mask. Lance's face was still blue, red, and lumpy.

They tried a wig. It wasn't enough.

"Try a hat," said Gladys. "A really big one."

"That's good," said Beauty. "With the right gown, he'll be stunning."

"You're not getting me into a skirt," said Lance.

"You wanna wear a skirt or a roasting pan?" Gladys asked. "Your choice."

Lance gulped. But even dressed up, Lance was still partly eggsposed.

"Your tail feathers have to be tweezed," Beauty said. "They're a dead giveaway."

"Not my glorious tail feathers," whined Lance.

"Roast turkey with chestnut dressing . . . ," Gladys reminded him.

Lance moaned. "Start plucking."

It took the whole day to
complete Lance's makeover.
Then Beauty stayed up all night
trying to assure Lance that the
disguise would save him,
even though she wasn't at all
convinced herself.

The next day the farmer and his wife came for the turkey.

"You let him escape, Sam. You've ruined Thanksgiving dinner."

Sam spotted Lance. "Let's roast that plump hen, Ethel."

Lance trembled. Beauty held her breath.

"Thanksgiving without turkey, Sam? No way! We're all going out to a restaurant." So Sam and Ethel left, and Lance was safe.

Lance slowly adjusted to his new life. He enjoyed the Scratching in the Garden Club and the weekly Chickers tournament. Lance became Beauty's biggest customer, with regular appointments for tail feather waxing.

Beauty continued to give Lance lessons,
trying to get his flying skills up to scratch.

One day while Beauty was giving Hattie a perm, she asked, "Lance, would you like to go back to being a turkey?"

"Yes," Lance admitted. "But even if I get away, a skirt, blouse, and bonnet will always be my Thanksgiving dressing."